FOR MATT

**About the story**

Bogles were believed to be wicked goblin-like creatures
that lived in the marshlands and swamps of the UK. This story is a retelling
of an old English folktale that has its roots in the Lincolnshire fens.
Also known as THE BOGLES AND THE MOON and THE DEAD MOON, it was probably first told
to young children to scare them away from the dangerous Lincolnshire marshlands.
The first time the story appeared in print was in 1891
in LEGENDS OF THE LINCOLNSHIRE CARS
by Mrs M.C. Balfour.

First published in Great Britain in 2004 by
Frances Lincoln Children's Books, 4 Torriano Mews, Torriano Avenue, London NW5 2RZ
www.franceslincoln.com

Distributed in the USA by Publishers Group West

British Library Cataloguing in Publication Data available on request

ISBN 1-84507-095-X

Printed in Singapore

1 3 5 7 9 8 6 4 2

# THE MOON
# IN SWAMPLAND

Retold and illustrated
by M.P. Robertson

FRANCES LINCOLN CHILDREN'S BOOKS

he stars were always telling the Moon

about the dark deeds that went on in Swampland

whenever her back was turned.

One night she said, "I'll see for myself."

She put on human form, and shrouding her silver hair

in a cloak of night, she glided down to earth.

The Moon landed on a path winding between murky pools.

The only light came from Will-o'-the-Wisps, who tried to lure her

from the safety of the path with the eerie glow

of their lanterns.

The Moon picked her way through the shadows.

She saw vague shapes lurking in the mist.

She heard horrible squelchings and evil belchings.

When she wandered too close to the water's edge,

clammy, webbed fingers snatched at her cloak.

The bogles were hungry tonight!

The Moon skipped lightly from stone to tussock until,

tripping over a loose rock, she grabbed at a clump

of reeds to steady herself. The reeds coiled

around her wrists. She tugged and twisted,

but the more she tugged, the tighter

the reeds held her.

As the Moon struggled, she heard the cry of a child.

A boy had been led astray by Will-o'-the-Wisps. He was stumbling
through the stinking quagmire, with creeping horrors plucking at his coat.

Summoning the last of her strength, the Moon shook off her hood.
Light streamed from her silver hair, lighting up the swamp as if it were day.

The bogles ran screeching for cover.

Now the boy could see the path clearly,

and headed for home.

The Moon was exhausted. She bowed her head and the hood slipped
forward again, covering her hair.

Now the bogles could see her clearly. They came creeping out
of their lairs, cackling with glee.

They dragged the Moon into their deepest, darkest bog-hole,
blocked the entrance with a heavy boulder,
and slimed their way back to their hovels.

Days turned into weeks, and weeks into months.
As dreary night followed dreary night, the townsfolk
began to wonder why the Moon had abandoned them.
No one dared to go into the dark swamp.

As the bogles grew bolder, they began to venture
into the town. At night the townsfolk kept
their doors locked and their lanterns
burning bright, for they knew that if their fires
went out, the bogles would come in.

One evening, the desperate townsfolk gathered in the tavern. Why had the Moon abandoned them? Was the Earth about to fall from the heavens? Was it a witch's curse?

Then a young boy called Thomas shouted above the noise.

"I know where the Moon is!" he said.

"You?" said the landlord. "You're just a boy! It was you who got lost in the swamp and came back looking like one of those horrible creatures."

But everyone listened as Thomas told them about the night he had been lost in the swamp, and how he had been saved by a mysterious light.

"I think it was the Moon who saved me," said Thomas. "Perhaps she is a prisoner of the bogles."

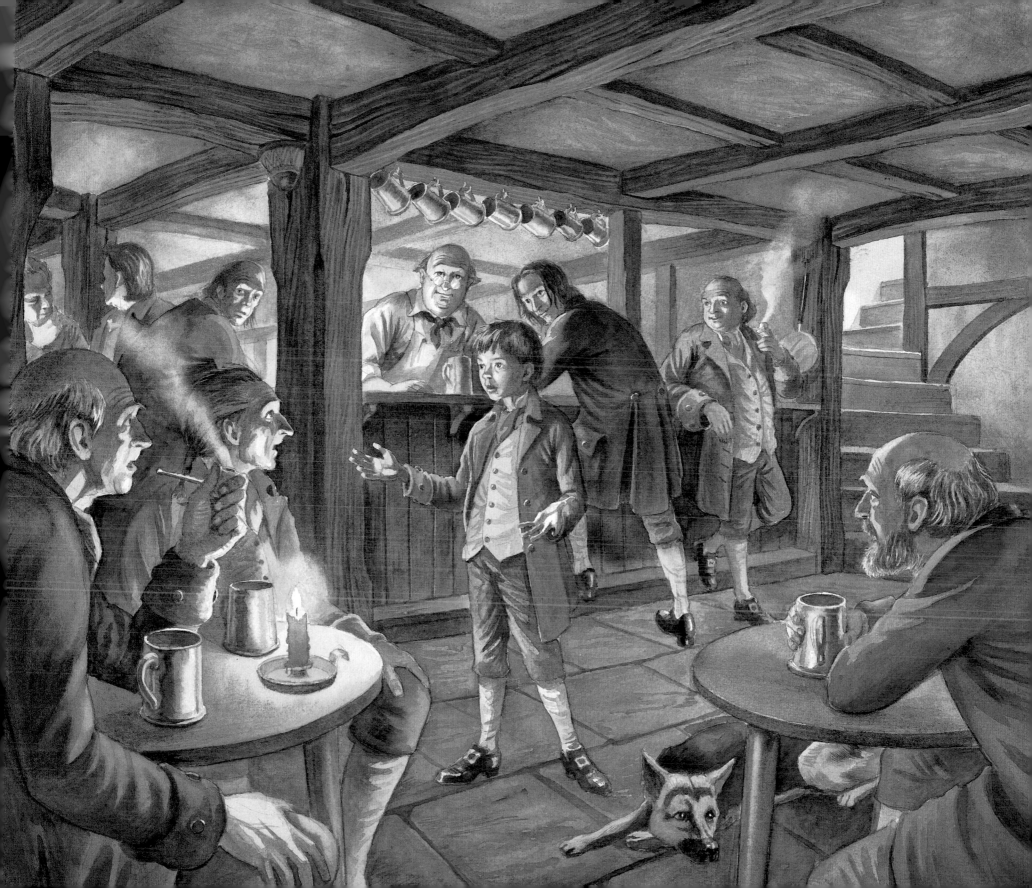

They decided to ask the advice of the wise old woman
who lived at the mill.

Armed with pitchforks and brandishing torches,
they marched boldly up through the village
and knocked at her door.

The old woman looked
at them. "You won't scare
bogles away with the courage
of fools," she said.

Then she beckoned
them inside.

When she heard Thomas's story, the old woman
scratched her hairy chin. She consulted a dusty book
and looked into her crystal ball.

"What do you see?" asked Thomas.

"Darkness," she replied.

The old woman looked deeper into her crystal ball.

"Now, this is what you must do…"

Later that night, Thomas led a line of men across the swamp.

Each man was holding on tightly to the shoulder of the man in front.

They could see nothing, but they sensed the evil lying in wait

and their hearts were icy with fear.

At last they came across a great boulder,
lying half-submerged in a gloomy pool.

The men threw open their coats to reveal blazing
lanterns hidden beneath, and held them high
in the darkness. Howling, the bogles fled from the light.

The men worked quickly to move the boulder
and finally rolled it away. As the muddy water cleared,
a strange and haunting face appeared. Its beauty
touched every heart.

Luckily Thomas kept his wits about him. He plunged into the freezing water. He hacked through the tangled reeds and fought his way to where the Moon lay.

Then he cut the ties that bound her.

There was a blinding flash and, like a comet, the Moon soared back
into the heavens. She lit a bright path home for her rescuers,
and drove the bogles down into the darkest depths of their slimy mire.

And from that day to this, the Moon has remained in the sky.
So if you have to travel through Swampland at night, make sure
the Moon is shining brightly – lighting up the shadows where
the dark things wait.